MW00413215

SIBYLS

SIBYLS

Copyright © 2020 Melissa Bobe
All rights reserved.
ISBN-13: 9781657203112

A Hive Press Book

Cover photograph by Joshua Fuller on unsplash.com
Cover design by Melissa Bobe

To my fellow creatives
with gratitude
for the encouragement and inspiration

The road is long
and has been made much brighter
by your company

SIBYLS

A Novella

Melissa Bobe

THE HIVE PRESS

I.

Foreston was a small and quiet town. It had been such for as long as its sparse population could recall, and what they didn't remember, they didn't question. So when the twelve-day rain arrived, there wasn't more than a murmur of complaint from the residents, perhaps because that was their way, or perhaps because they could not know that the unusual weather was to alter their small town forever—or, at least, for as long as they would live to see.

The rain wasn't heavy and it wasn't violent. It could hardly be called a storm, really, though the damage it yielded compelled town residents to refer to it as such in the weeks to follow. But as they were to discover, twelve days of steady rain was just long enough to ruin everything a little bit.

Homes weren't flooded or swept away, but after the rain had passed, they never quite dried out. Roofs didn't cave in, but instead swelled beneath shingles warped by moisture that set itself deep between wood and stone. Linens sagged clammy on clotheslines, flags fell limp on breezy days, and awnings above local storefronts lost their tension. And beneath the feet of the Foreston residents, water had moved far into the ground, invisible to them but nevertheless changing the very foundations on which they lived.

Twelve days didn't drown a town, but it did invite a constant damp that you couldn't put your finger on, though it followed you wherever you went. A chill had entered each and every Foreston dwelling, and it would not leave no matter how the residents wrapped themselves in blankets, lit up their fireplaces, or raised the heat in their homes. The town survived, but it was never dry again.

Melissa Bobe

II.

Some will say that a place is only as strange as its strangest citizen. Foreston's local oddity was Artinand, an unmarried tinker and clockmaker of sorts. Skilled as he was at fixing metal gears and wheels—the smaller the machine, the more precise his work—Artinand's claim to local fame came in the form of ceramics: small figurines shaped in the likeness of women that he crafted meticulously and hated with all of his being. He called them sibyls.

The sibyls were never intended to be sold, though sell throughout the town they did. Unbeknownst to his neighbors, Artinand had crafted the sibyls in an effort to gain a certain kind of foresight, a glimpse of things yet to come. As he painstakingly shaped, set, and painted each miniature woman, Artinand commanded that she give him whatever futuresight he desired.

He was fickle enough, never seeming to settle on a particular vision of the future; or perhaps it was that he was greedy. One sibyl was formed to reveal matters of the heart. Another was built to sense trouble that lay ahead. Yet another he'd created to predict storms, not unlike the one that had lingered in Foreston for nearly a fortnight.

But well-made as the sibyls were, they did not yield the results their maker demanded. Though he'd certainly mastered the art of bringing the small ceramic women into being, he couldn't glean from them the knowledge he was convinced they must possess. Assuming them to be as selfish as he himself was, Artinand subjected the figurines to muttered insults and wild rants of frustration. His livid face, red with rage, was the first thing their silent, frozen countenances met with as the glaze upon them dried.

Soon enough, patrons coming in with broken watches and music boxes began to notice the figurines around the shop. If they were curious to behold, the craftsmanship with which they'd been so carefully made seemed to more than make up for it. Before long, customers were asking about a price; and, disgusted that his creations would not give him what he desired, Artinand sold all of them to the townspeople. It became something of a local novelty to have a sibyl on one's mantle or windowsill, and after they'd all been purchased, several Foreston residents expressed regret at not having moved more quickly to buy.

By the time the twelve-day rain arrived, Artinand had made and sold a good twenty sibyls, barely able to contain his sneers as he sent them away. Never did it occur to him that something might be lacking on his end, that perhaps his creations' reluctance to share their prophetic ways could be due to his manner of asking. He considered himself lucky to be rid of each one as she found herself a home somewhere in the town.

During the rain, Artinand found it impossible to work at all. The silence of stopped clocks persisted, necklace chains remained broken and strewn about his worktable, and his workshop was in a general state of disarray. The thing that stopped him from working was the constancy of the rain; the sound seemed to enter his very mind and kept him from focusing on anything beyond his own failings, the passage of his life moving along at a rate he could do nothing to slow.

And when the rain had finally stopped, he'd lost the will to craft another sibyl at all, and he packed the tools with which to make them away in a drawer, swearing that each and every one of his ungrateful creations had left him with spite in her ceramic heart.

III.

Adjusting to the new climate of the town was a challenge. Local agriculture was affected, as was the town infrastructure: roads seemed to sink at random, lampposts and telephone poles tilted so that none stood straight, and before long, it became clear that no dry weather plants could survive in the soil of Foreston.

The church tower's bells sang a muted song such that they no longer woke the town on Sunday mornings; only those living close by heard the sound at all, and rather than rousing them from sleep, it merely played quietly in their dreams. Dawn seemed coated with a haze that kept the sun from bursting in through windows, and the stars were obscured in the night sky so that by late evening, darkness above the town was complete.

Thus, the period after the storm necessitated quiet adjustments which preoccupied all occupants of the town. In the midst of getting acclimated to the new conditions of their streets and homes, the citizens of Foreston neglected to notice another change that the storm had left in its wake. This change was small, but significant.

Something was missing from twenty Foreston households: twenty small objects that had been beautifully handcrafted but were easy enough to overlook, especially amidst an effort to dry out soggy, sagging homes.

Over the course of the twelve days of steady, unceasing rain, each and every sibyl in Foreston had vanished, leaving no reminder of her existence behind.

IV.

Cecelia Orton woke gasping in the early hours of the morning, terrified for her youngest daughter. Her husband grumbled awake, demanding to know what was the matter, but by the time he'd blinked his eyes, he was alone in their room. Cecelia had run to her children's bedroom before another breath could escape her.

She found her son and two daughters resting peacefully; the youngest, Ivra, even smiled in her sleep. Cecelia tried futilely to calm her racing heart. It was as though some horrible knowledge deep inside of her was insisting she hear it out.

"Ivra." She grabbed her daughter's hands, thinking that maybe if Ivra spoke to her, her fear would subside.

"What's wrong with you?" her husband whispered, swaying groggily in the doorway of the children's room.

"Ivra, my baby." She ignored him. Let him wonder what was wrong with her. She didn't have time to wonder; she had to know if her child was all right.

"Mommy?" The small girl opened her eyes, confused to find her mother's hand on her forehead. "What's wrong, Mommy?"

"Are you okay?"

Ivra yawned. "I was dreaming about eating chocolate."

Cecelia smiled automatically at her daughter's sleepy words. But the terror gnawing at her heart persisted, even after her husband shooed her away from Ivra, who quickly fell back to sleep.

The next day passed without incident, her husband only remarking briefly on his wife's strange behavior before he left for work. Cecelia did her best to clean the house, care for the kids, and busy her hands throughout the afternoon to distract herself from that strange fear she still felt.

That evening, dinner would have been typical if she weren't so quiet. Her husband seemed to want to ask what was bothering her, but chose to speak with the children instead. His wife barely touched her food.

Just before dawn the next day, their older daughter cried out mere seconds after Cecelia had again sat upright and jumped out of bed.

"What now?" Her husband woke more quickly this morning, given the plaintive tone of their daughter's calls.

Both parents rushed to the children's room, Cecelia leading the way. Ivra was moaning in bed, her skin burning to the touch, and vomit was strewn across the top of her comforter.

When the town doctor, who made emergency home visits, had finished his exam, he glanced up at Ivra's parents standing anxiously by, holding one another as the light of early morning glowed through the windows of the damp, cold house.

"It's a good thing you didn't wait on this," he told them. "This looks like a normal flu bug, but without help, she would have been much worse by evening. We would have probably ended up at the hospital instead. How did you know to call me right away?"

Cecelia felt herself exhale for the first time in two days; the awful, grating fear that had kept her on edge was gone as suddenly as it had overtaken her. But she found that she had no answer for the doctor, because she didn't understand how or why she had known something was wrong with her daughter.

"Mother's intuition, I suppose," her husband replied, giving credit where it was due and squeezing his wife's hand to let her know he was sorry to have doubted her.

But since when had intuition come in the form of a terror that would not leave?

V.

Yvonne Argos woke to find her sister's weaving dispersed about the entirety of their home, bizarre tunnels of brightly colored yarn that seemed as useless as they were many. It looked as though she had been working all night.

"Margery, what is all of this?"

But her sister, sitting at the small loom in the corner of her bedroom, blinked at her as though she were still asleep.

"What are you making?" Yvonne pressed, a little bewildered by Margery's unresponsive expression. It wasn't like her sister to work through the night.

"Oh," Margery remarked, seeming to notice the loom in front of her for the very first time. Then she shrugged and continued working with the pile of yarn in her lap.

Yvonne had always been the more cautious of the two and would have called the doctor regarding Margery's condition, but she had errands to run and it was still early. She thought that, by the time she returned home, Margery might come to her senses.

But when she finally did arrive back at their apartment, Yvonne found Margery folding the tunnels of woven yarn into small, neat squares and stacking them on the sitting room table.

"Working on something in particular?"

Margery only shrugged once more, then asked, "Fish for lunch?"

The week passed, and the pile of yarn tunnels continued to grow. Margery didn't seem tight-lipped on the subject so much as just plain confused by her own creations, as her sister also continued to be.

That Friday morning, they received a phone call.

"Hello?"

"Is that Yvonne or Margery?"

"It's Yvonne," she responded, recognizing the anxious tones of the local elementary school secretary's voice. "Is everything all right, Mary?"

"Oh, yes," Mary answered, not sounding all right by any estimate. "It's just that the children's dance for the bonanza tomorrow might not work out. The rain seeped into the closet where we'd kept all of the costumes, you see, and they were mostly cardboard, so there's hardly anything left of them."

"I'm sorry to hear that," Yvonne said, truly feeling bad for the woman. The rain had caused so many unexpected problems around town. "But what can we do? You know Margery can't make anything that quickly. How many children is it for?"

"Thirty-two," Mary told her mournfully.

"Costumes for over thirty children? No, I don't see how we can…" Yvonne trailed off as her eye caught the colorful pile of folded yarn resting on the sitting room table.

"Yvonne? Did I lose you?"

"Just…just give me a moment…" She was silently counting the folded squares her sister had stacked together. There were exactly thirty-one.

"Margie? Can you come out here, dear?" Yvonne called her sister, then spoke into the phone again. "I…can hardly believe it, Mary, but we might be able to help you, after all."

A hopeful gasp and a volley of gratitude sounded over the phone as Margery came out of her room, a colorful woven garment in her hands. "I just had to finish up," she told her sister as she added it to the pile.

"We'll come by the school this afternoon." Yvonne's placid tone did not betray her astonishment, but her eyes were wide as she hung up the phone.

"What's wrong?" Margery asked, puzzled by her sister's expression.

"How did you know the children were going to need costumes?"

"Costumes? What children?"

At a loss for words, Yvonne gestured to the stacks of folded yarn.

"Oh!" Relief passed across Margery's face. "That's what they are. Well, I'm glad to know they'll go to good use."

"Yes, but *how*—"

Her sister sighed and shrugged for the umpteenth time that week. "Yvonne, don't ask me questions I can't answer. Do you feel like some tea before we head over to the school?"

She filled the kettle and put it on the stove. The flame flickered, something it had only started to do after the twelve days of rain, as though it had to struggle in order to stay lit.

VI.

"Grandma, please don't leave the house today. Something bad is going to happen."

Neve Hobbs looked at her son sharply. "Billy, what a thing to say to your grandmother! Apologize!"

Her mother chuckled indulgently. "Let the boy speculate, Neve. What's going to happen to an old bat in the middle of the day?"

"Please, Grandma." He reached across the table to grasp her hand. "Stay home. I'll stay with you—I don't feel like going to school."

"Oh, is that it?" His mother snorted. "Nice try. You're going to school, mister. Threatening your grandmother isn't going to get you out of it."

"No, it's not that…" He frowned, having difficulty articulating what it was that he was trying to warn them about. He slid his plate away from him, his breakfast barely touched, and let out a small sigh.

"I think you're actually worried," his grandmother remarked, noting the conflict on his face. "Don't be, my dear. I'll be just fine. I'm only headed to Ella Samson's up the street. Her husband threw out his back, and she'll need some help around the house until he's on his feet again."

"As long as you don't throw your own back out in the process," her daughter advised. "Ella Samson has three children to help her, you know."

"And all three of them left town a long time ago, Neve. You know that; I didn't raise you to be uncharitable."

"You didn't raise me to be taken advantage of, either. When's the last time Ella did you a favor?"

"Mom," Billy tried again, "I can help Mrs. Samson after school. Just let Grandma stay home today."

His mother smiled at him now. "I guess you aren't just plotting to cut school. But Billy, Grandma's right—nothing's going to happen to her today. She's only headed up the street. If it makes you feel better, you can always meet her there after school and walk her home."

And just like that, it was time to leave for school and work and Mrs. Samson's, so the household went their separate ways. Billy spent a frustrated morning with his worries. He even tried approaching his homeroom teacher, but when she asked what exactly was the matter, he found it impossible to answer her. It felt like the longest day he'd ever spent, worrying about his grandmother and wanting nothing but to head back home and be with her.

School finally ended. Walking from the bus stop towards his house, Billy saw the lights of the sheriff's truck flashing. He tore forward, his feet propelling the rest of him, which was sinking somewhere deep and dark. The ambulance that sped in from behind him passed Billy halfway down the street, winning a race that he'd known all day he was destined to lose.

He arrived to find his mother deep in conversation with the sheriff, who had a comforting hand on her shoulder as they spoke. "Mom! What happened?"

His mother's face was wet with tears, and she shook her head. "Oh, sweetie." She reached out as if to embrace him, but suddenly her tears stopped and her face went pale. "Billy...honey, how did you know Grandma should stay home today?"

"Ma'am?" the sheriff asked her, glancing uncertainly between Neve and Billy.

"He knew," she told the sheriff, shaking her head. "Billy somehow knew...He said this morning that she needed to stay home. Did someone you know tell you this was going to happen, Billy? Someone from school?"

"What are you talking about?" he asked plaintively. "Mom, what happened? Where's Grandma?"

Relief spread through his mother's eyes. "No, you couldn't have known," she murmured, half to herself. Then she pulled him into a hug. "Billy, I'm so sorry. Grandma's going to need to go to the hospital right now—that's why the ambulance is here. She and Mrs. Samson, they were...attacked. Someone tried to hurt them."

"Is Grandma going to be okay?"

"They're going to help her out in the ambulance, son," the sheriff said. "Now, you knew something about this?"

Billy shook his head. "I just knew that Grandma should stay home today, but I didn't know why." He suddenly grew angry. "Why would somebody hurt them? They're just two old ladies."

"The Samson's place was almost robbed," the sheriff answered. "Word must have gotten around that John had thrown his back out and Ella would be home alone with him." He smirked. "Well, alone except for your grandmother."

"Grandma's not hurt bad?"

His mother sighed. "She's going to live, but they did rough her up a bit. There were two attackers, and they're big men."

Billy frowned at the sheriff. "What are you laughing at, then?"

"I didn't mean to laugh, Billy." The sheriff gave a shrug, still smiling. "Thing is, your grandmother probably saved Ella Samson's life. She beat the hell out of the robbers—I've got them both in the back of my truck, and I'm wondering if I'm not going to have to drive them to the hospital before jail."

Billy felt himself relax a little. "Really?"

The sheriff nodded reassuringly. "Your grandma's first words when I arrived on the scene were: 'You should see the other guys.'"

The ambulance was turning up the street again now, his grandmother and Mrs. Samson inside. Billy turned to his mother. "Can we go with her to the hospital?"

Neve nodded. "Yeah, let's get in the car and follow them. You have everything you need from me?" she asked the sheriff.

"Yes, ma'am. I'll come by in a day or so to check on your mother." He smiled again. "And maybe to ask her to join our neighborhood watch, along with your son here and his good instincts."

His mother patted Billy's back, and he knew she meant by the gesture that she was proud of him. All he wanted, though, was to be at his grandmother's side, and he was silent during the ride to the hospital.

VII.

By the time Mark Templeton got home from work, he was too exhausted to make any real efforts at dinner beyond a beer. He threw down the empty bottle after he'd drained it and collapsed onto the bed, knowing his wife had left for her night shift at the diner an hour or so before he'd arrived home.

It had been a more exciting day than he was used to, what with the Huang twins calling first thing in the morning and insisting that they'd known every meal every neighbor within a stone's throw would be eating for breakfast, lunch, and dinner that day before anyone had even turned on their stove. "Except the Argos sisters—they won't be having lunch at all, only tea. We don't know why, but we shouldn't even know that! You've got to do something, sheriff."

Then Lydia Singh had come in, insisting that he do something about the fence that would be vandalized downtown later the following week: "I can't tell you *how* or *who*, Mark. Just do something about it! My nephew was one of the guys who put it up last month. Bad enough the rain's made everything crooked. We don't need vandalism to make things any uglier around here."

And then there was the break-in over at the Samson house. Since his first day as sheriff, he hadn't had so much excitement—at least, not professionally. He thought fondly of Adriana and the thrill he'd felt when they had started seeing each other almost half a year ago. That was a whole other mess, though one he was only somewhat sorry to be in.

"It's time, baby," she'd said the last evening they'd spent together. "You've got to tell your wife about us."

"Tell her?" He'd shaken his head. "Adriana, she thinks I'm pulling overtime, that I'm out there catching bad guys, right now, right this minute. What am I supposed to tell her?"

"That it's over."

Adriana didn't mince words; it was how their affair had started and escalated so quickly. She was too direct to get to know little by little, and he'd wanted it all from the moment they'd met.

"I can't, not yet."

She frowned. "Why the hell not?"

"I don't know. I don't want to…destroy someone's life."

He sighed now as he thought about it, kicking his shoes off and pulling the covers over him. He'd meant what he'd said—he didn't want to destroy Miranda. And she would never even see it coming, poor thing. She was so sweet and trusting, which was why he'd fallen in love with her in the first place. They'd built a life together, and she worked as hard as he did—maybe harder, if he was going to be honest about it. Just because his heart wasn't in their marriage anymore didn't mean that she deserved to have her world turned upside down.

Sleep drew him away from this conflicted state of mind not long after he was under the covers. Then, in the early hours of the morning, he felt a shift in the silence of the house. And he saw it, though his eyes were closed and he still lay in bed: the barrel of his own shotgun, pointed directly at his body in the darkness. It wasn't possible, but there it was in his mind, clear as day: gunmetal shining under mute, soft moonlight, steady, ready, and undeniable.

He rolled off the bed just as the shot went off.

"Miranda! What the—"

"I've had enough, Mark!" Miranda's voice rang out shriller than he'd ever heard it. "Enough of you and your slut!"

Another shot, another dodge, just seconds before it hit its target.

"Miranda, please! I—I don't want to arrest you!"

She shrieked with laughter in the dark as he tackled the gun from her, a deranged laugh he was accustomed to hearing from drunks and lunatics. "Arrest me! As if that's the worst thing you could do! You fucking bastard!"

As the first rays of sunlight began peeking through Foreston, Mark found himself back at the station, his wife in handcuffs, his marriage in shambles. But all he could think was: how? How was it that he'd known the shotgun was aimed at him? How could he roll off the bed in time to save his own life, knowing what would happen well before it did?

VIII.

It didn't take long for news of the precognitive abilities that were manifesting among the residents of Foreston to reach the edges of town. Soon after the twelve-day rain—just as its effects were becoming an accepted part of everyday life—it became clear that nearly every household in Foreston held at least one person who was able to glimpse that which was to come.

When Artinand heard about the phenomenon, a wild bitterness rose in his heart. Deep down, he knew this was the work of the sibyls, *his* sibyls, traitorous and selfish ceramic bitches that they were. He was livid that they had dispersed across Foreston what was rightfully his, these abilities that had been squandered on his neighbors, the buffoonish, the simple-minded, and the unremarkable alike.

But for the moment, he had no idea where the sibyls were. He hadn't cared to which homes they had gone when he'd sold them; indeed, he'd avoided getting to know Foreston as much as possible, only heading into the heart of town when completely necessary. But had he spoken to his neighbors about the ceramic oddities he'd sold them, they wouldn't have had much information to offer. As household objects, the sibyls weren't particularly large or obtrusive; each stood half a foot tall and blended easily on top of mantles and in cabinets along with other ornaments. And so when they'd vanished, no one had noticed. After all, the town residents had been a little preoccupied with seeing the future and cleaning up after the rain.

From what little he'd heard, the psychic gifts of the sibyls were being used in foolish, insignificant ways, for glimpses of the future that meant little to anyone but the small lives into which they'd manifested. And knowing that, Artinand felt himself mocked as well as cheated by his creations. Lurking about his workshop in his usual embittered solitude, he cursed them and swore his eventual revenge.

There was no one to tell Artinand that, while his instincts about where the precognitive abilities around town had come from were pretty much on the mark, his ideas about revenge missed it by a long shot. No one could say to him that, gripped by his sweaty, meaty hands, each sibyl had feared being thrown back into the kiln after he'd created her, one of many threats he'd muttered in his rages over being denied the gift of precognition. No one was there to remind him that he'd brought his figurines into being with nothing but nastiness in word and tone. No one could point out that, with a maker like him, it wasn't Artinand who was entitled to revenge. And no one was there to let him know that revenge was exactly what was beginning, but only just.

The sibyls were many things: small, prescient, clairvoyant, beautiful. But forgiveness was not something they were inclined towards. They had the memory of any enchanted object, which was long and focused, limited to how they had been handled and for what they had been used.

Products of the home from which they came, the sibyls were so many things: clever as they were prophetic, dangerous as they were lovely, and merciless as the man who'd made them.

IX.

Unusual though the decision was in the wake of such a violent act, Miranda Templeton was released from jail on the conditions that she continue going to work, not flee the area, and find somewhere else to live. And that she not attempt to kill her husband again.

Mark had decided not to press charges in his capacity as both the town sheriff and her cheating chickenshit of a husband. He spun some story to the rest of the precinct about her having her nights confused and thinking there was an intruder in their bed. She didn't say a word the entire time, knowing that she could only land herself behind bars, and that would hardly allow her the pleasure of murdering his lying, unfaithful ass, which she still intended to do.

She felt like garbage by the time she got to her friend Amy's apartment. She chalked it up to spending the night in a jail cell, but nevertheless threw up the moment she arrived.

"You all right?" Amy called through the bathroom door.

"Garbage," Miranda moaned, puking again.

Amy waited a beat, then told her, "I'm putting out clean sheets and a change of clothes on the guest bed for you. There's a pregnancy test under the sink if you need it, and antacids in the medicine cabinet if you don't."

Miranda laughed. That would be rich, wouldn't it? Pregnant and soon-to-be-divorced with a loser, cheater husband. But another wave of nausea cut her laughter short.

She sat with a thump on Amy's bathroom floor, thinking. When was she supposed to get her period? Was it this week, or last?

Not bothering to get up off the floor, she slid over on her rear to the cabinet underneath the sink. It didn't take much rifling around to find the box of pregnancy tests. It was open and one had already been used—Amy must have had a recent scare herself.

Miranda pulled the remaining test out and matter-of-factly reviewed the instructions on the folded pamphlet inside of the box. These things were all basically the same, but she didn't want to risk misinformation. Her day was going badly enough as it was.

She stared at the test in her hand, its cheerful pastel purple inciting yet another flicker of nausea. Should she even bother? She couldn't actually be pregnant, could she? They'd stopped trying nearly a year ago, when she'd picked up the night shift at the diner.

But what if she was? That feeling washed over her again, that blinding, hot-white senselessness that had helped her load the shotgun and fire it. It lulled Miranda, soothing the whir of thoughts and emotions running rampant inside her. And it said that a pregnancy, well: what better revenge could there be?

She knew she should feel some pull of the maternal, that she should be thinking of the child that would ultimately come after a pregnancy. But all she saw in her mind at the moment was that little skank her husband had been fucking for who knew how many months.

Mark was well liked in town, at the top of his career, and could easily marry again. For Miranda, though, a divorce would represent an ending of sorts, something she might not come back from. It wouldn't matter that she'd grown up in Foreston and that there should be some regard for her, too, among neighbors and friends. Like it or not, the situation came down to the way things fell with men as opposed to with women, and to deny that would just be plain stupid.

If she was pregnant, though, she'd have claim to something. She'd be able to get money, some help for the baby, and she'd have been someone's wife in a way that demanded recognition—not just a ship that had passed in the night while he screwed around town, looking to do it right the second time.

If Mark thought he'd get away from her with no strings attached, he'd have to think again. That is, if she was pregnant. If.

She struggled to her feet and sat on the toilet, unwrapping the test with steady hands.

X.

Eliot Bronston didn't know what to make of the week he'd just had. Sure, the incidence of precognition after the twelve-day rain had meant he'd had to reevaluate things. As the Foreston family doctor, he'd humbled himself; a man of science by trade, he'd nevertheless allowed his neighbors to educate him in folk remedies over the years. This was in no small part because he'd rather parse those homeopathic efforts, pointing his patients from the supposed cures that were dangerous and towards the ones that were perhaps lightly effective, or at least innocuous in their uselessness.

And as a man of science, psychic provenance wasn't something he'd been particularly open to. However, after seeing one family after another have incidents, and then his own wife, of course—it was difficult to argue with all of that. Speculation was one thing, but these were things to which he himself had borne witness. And after all, there was no progress to be had in science if one couldn't accept that an anomaly had become a shift in paradigms.

He wasn't a psychologist in any sense, and so he allowed that things had changed, in terms of what the human mind might do, at least within town limits. And for the most part it seemed as though the outbreak of precognition had dissipated for the moment, to the relief of many, including Eliot.

But things like pregnancy were supposed to fall in his wheelhouse, so to speak, and Eliot didn't appreciate being blown away by phenomena within the purview of his practice. It undermined patient confidence in the doctor, he was sure; worse, it undermined his confidence in himself.

"Twenty women," he said to his secretary. "In the same week, twenty women confirmed newly pregnant! I know some couples might have spent more time at home together than usual during the twelve-day rain, but…twenty!" He couldn't stop repeating the number.

Ruth shook her head, then smiled a little wistfully. "I remember my first. I was so scared that some kind of complication might happen. Thank goodness I had you, Dr. Bronston! It turned out to be a wonderful pregnancy."

"I appreciate that, Ruth," he told her warmly, but quickly returned to the anxiety at hand. "The thing is, I can't support twenty women who all seem to be in the same stage—if not the same week—of pregnancy at the same time."

"How's that, doctor?"

"Simple numbers—there's one of me and twenty of them. We're going to be overwhelmed with the check-ups! The ultrasounds and consultations and false labor alarms, and—my god, Ruth, I didn't even think of it, but they're all due at the same time! What if there are multiple deliveries in the same day?"

Ruth shrugged, not one to panic until it was really time to panic. "I suppose…couldn't the hospital help out with that?"

He nodded, trying to be patient with her lack of alarm. "Of course, they have the facilities to care for these women. But I'm the family doctor, Ruth. I'm supposed to deliver them and then deliver their kids twenty years later. It's not right for me not to be present at the births."

He was trying not to fret; the urge to wring his hands was overwhelming. "Besides, hospitals are clinical. Pregnant women don't like them, especially when I've made myself available for so many home births. It's what the community expects."

"Well, doctor, I'm sure help will come, somehow. It always does, if you keep the faith long and strong enough."

"Let's hope you're right, Ruth."

XI.

"Marie, just please tell me: why is the car on fire?" Theo was struggling not to shout, but given the flames flickering across the leather upholstery of a car he'd spent the past several years fixing up, it was something of a losing battle.

"You love that piece of shit more than me!" Marie, on the other hand, was clearly fine with shouting. "More than me, and more than this child we're about to bring into the world!"

"Baby, that is not true! I love you so much I can't even put it into words, but…I've gotta call the fire department! This is cr—"

"You had *damn well* better not be about to call me crazy, Theo! I swear, I'll set you on fire next!"

Theo didn't doubt it. At this point, he was at a complete loss as to how to handle Marie. Since she'd gotten pregnant, she had been more volatile than his childhood family guard dog after the poor thing had gotten dementia. And as far as he could tell, Marie was a hell of a lot more dangerous.

"I *fucking*" —WHACK!— "*hate*" —WHACK!— "this car!"

She'd taken up a two-by-four and was now beating the trunk of the car, apparently not content with having already set the interior on fire.

"Marie, we've got to get out of here! There's gasoline in there—it could explode!"

"You'd better hope *I* don't explode!" she told him, but finally allowed herself to be coaxed indoors, two-by-four still in hand.

Theo waited until she'd raged into another room, then opened the fridge and downed half a beer. It was one of only two things getting him through, at this point: beer, and the knowledge that he was definitely not alone. One of his buddies had a pregnant wife at home, too. They were expecting around the same time Theo and Marie were, and his friend's wife was apparently no picnic at the moment, either. He didn't know if she'd also started setting things on fire, but his friend had told him that most days he came home to his wife throwing things at him. Heavy things.

It didn't seem normal to Theo. Sure, pregnant women had hormone shifts or whatever it was that gave them mood swings, but he'd never heard of lethal behavior. And it wasn't just him and his friend. There were rumors around town about a surge in pregnancies, about everyone being due at around the same time, and about the expectant mothers driving everyone else out of their minds.

Theo blamed the twelve-day rain. The town hadn't been the same since, and neither had anyone in it, as far as he was concerned. First, it was that weird psychic shit he'd heard people talking about, and now all these women getting knocked up at the same time? What were the odds of that?

The fire department didn't even seem surprised when he called and explained the situation. "Pregnant, huh?" the operator said, then promised a truck would be by as soon as possible. At this point, it seemed like everyone in Foreston was anticipating these outbursts and adjusting accordingly. He had to hand it to his town: it might be full of crazy shit, but people were surprisingly adaptable.

"Theo! Why the hell is there no hot water?"

He sighed, trudging back towards the bedroom, hoping that nothing else had been set aflame. At least the fire department was already en route, right?

XII.

"Okay, kids, back upstairs!"

"But we're gonna be late for school," Angela Ruiz-Keith protested.

"Late to school is better than dead at the hands of your mother."

Angela's younger brother, Nathan, shook his head. "She's *still* crazy?"

"Don't call Mama B crazy, Nathan," Xiomara said, ushering her grumbling children back up the stairs. "I think we've taught you better than to go around calling women crazy."

"Okay," Angela returned, hands on her narrow hips, "then how do you explain her shoving the air conditioners out the windows?"

"Or throwing away all of the food in the fridge?" Nathan chimed in.

"And don't forget about her putting the plants in the washing machi—"

"Enough!" Xiomara threw her hands up. "Obviously, Mama is having a tough time, and it's up to us to help take care of her. It's not easy being pregnant, and she needs our love and support. And patience."

Her daughter raised a dubious eyebrow at her. "Was it this hard being pregnant when she was having us?"

Glass shattered somewhere in the kitchen, and Nathan and Angela exchanged a glance.

"Stay here," Xiomara told them sternly. "Look, I'll even give you permission to watch some TV before school. Just give me a few minutes to handle this."

As she turned to go back down the stairs and see what her wife was up to now, Angela called after her, "Mami, please—we don't want to miss another full day."

A stab of guilt shot through Xiomara's stomach. It was all well and good to tell the kids not to worry about Brenna, but she was worried sick herself.

A knock sounded on the door as she was about to turn into the kitchen, and despite the sound of more glass breaking, Xiomara figured that whatever it was could wait a minute. She, like her children, was fast adjusting to everything in the house being a bit…different lately.

"Billy?" She was surprised to find Neve Hobbs's son standing on her doorstep. "What's up, sweetie? Is everything okay?"

"Yeah, Ms. Ruiz, I'm fine. I was just wondering if Angela and Nathan wanted to walk to school together. I have Angie's class notes from when she was out last week."

More guilt—she fought to smile at her neighbor's son. "You know what, Billy, the kids are probably going to miss first period today, so I don't think they'll be able to walk with you."

She could have tried to quickly usher them downstairs, but didn't want to risk Brenna coming out of the kitchen at the wrong moment. Separation anxiety seemed to be part of the household madness lately, and the last time Xiomara had tried to sneak the kids to school, she'd wound up with a screwdriver in her front tire.

There was another sudden crash from the kitchen, and Billy's face filled with alarm. "Are you guys okay, Ms. Ruiz?"

"Oh, we're good—nothing to worry about." Xiomara remembered now that the boy's grandmother had been involved in the Samson robbery somehow, and she asked, "Your grandma's doing okay, right?"

That brought a smile back to Billy's face. "She's great. I don't think anyone's going to try to rob the houses in our neighborhood anytime soon. Not after what she did to the robbers."

Chuckling, Xiomara asked, "Would you mind taking notes for Angie again during first period?" To the sound of further smashing, she added, "Maybe second period, too?"

Billy nodded. "Sure, Ms. Ruiz. See you soon!" And he ran off to school, clearly not wanting to stick around the chaos of the house any longer than he had to.

The question that Angela had raised earlier echoed through Xiomara's mind as she locked the front door. Why was this pregnancy so different? Sure, it was probably going to be their last kid, and Brenna wasn't quite as young as she'd been when they'd had Angela and Nathan. But Angie was barely in middle school—it hadn't been all *that* long ago, and age was only supposed to increase the risk of labor complications. There wasn't a single pregnancy book or website that had mentioned anything about homicidal tendencies. And Xiomara had definitely gone back to double-check her sources over the past few weeks.

"Did we get broken sperm?" she muttered to herself, hoping that the profile on their donor hadn't accidentally been swapped with a serial killer's. She started to feel guilty again, now for joining her son in thinking one of his moms had lost it, and then she entered the kitchen.

"Okay, so…we don't like glass anymore?" She knew she probably shouldn't have said anything: speaking to Brenna did not make things better whenever she was having one of these episodes. But it seemed as though, in the short time since she'd woken up, Brenna had managed to find every single glass item in their kitchen—from jars to cutting boards to wine glasses—and throw them all in a pile in the middle of the floor, where, of course, each item in question had shattered into an unholy mess.

Brenna looked at her, tearful as she often was in such moments, and Xiomara felt relief as she registered that, despite being still dressed in her nightgown and robe, her wife was wearing boots. They were wellies, actually, though why anyone would put on rain boots with her bathrobe…

But Xiomara had stopped asking why weeks ago. She had quickly learned that it didn't do any good, and everything she'd known about Brenna—how she was when she was pregnant, what to expect when they were expecting—well, all of it had gone out the window.

"You know, the kids have to go to school," she gently told her wife, watching as tears streamed down her face.

"I know."

"And we sort of have to…get them there."

Brenna gestured helplessly at the floor. "What about this?"

Xiomara sighed. "Well, thankfully Nathan and Angie haven't talked us into getting that dog they want so badly yet. It won't hurt anyone if we just leave it here for the time being."

Brenna didn't move, so Xiomara carefully tiptoed around the shards of glass between them and took her hand. "Want to come upstairs and get dressed?"

There was that distressed and distant look, the reluctance that was becoming so familiar as it moved across Brenna's face and even into her hand as Xiomara held it. Eventually, though, she let herself be led out of the kitchen and towards the stairs.

As they made their way back to their bedroom, Xiomara wondered again what could have caused such a drastically different pregnancy in this woman who had glowed through her first two, who on an ordinary day was unshakable in her good humor and levelheadedness.

But the ordinary had vanished from their lives, and Xiomara could only hope that it would return in a few months' time.

XIII.

Artinand continued to catch word of mischief he knew was the work of the sibyls. The stories of precognition had faded, and he guessed that they'd grown avaricious once more, stealing back their psychic prowess now that they'd sufficiently taunted him with the fleeting hints of the future they'd granted the townspeople. Damn it all, he never should have made the wretched things in the first place!

The gossip that reached him now had mostly to do with bizarre and violent behavior on the part of the Foreston women, which didn't interest him much beyond that he suspected his ingrate creations as its cause. He didn't know that the rumors had to do with twenty women in particular, nor did he catch wind of the fact that they all happened to be in a simultaneous stage of pregnancy. And the details might not have changed his feelings on the subject—women were acting unseemly to the extent that the morons of the town had begun scratching their near-empty heads over it. That was enough to implicate the sibyls, as far as he was concerned, and enough to incite him to begin plotting his revenge.

But Artinand was tucked in his bed, dreaming bitter dreams of his failures, when the town of Foreston was descended upon by twenty visitors moving silently through the dark of night. Most of the town was asleep upon their arrival, and so none witnessed their approach: twenty women shrouded in fine, flowing clothes with expressionless faces. Each stopped on the doorstep of a household where there was a woman expecting a child in a few months' time, and each waited patiently until morning to lift a knocker or ring a bell. And while the tenants of these homes may have been surprised to find a self-proclaimed midwife at their respective doors, they were more than that desperate and relieved to receive an offer of help—of *live-in* help, at that.

Had the pregnant women of Foreston been a bit less inclined towards arson, property destruction, and attempted murder, perhaps their loved ones might have thought twice about inviting strangers into their homes. Perhaps they would have scrutinized these newcomers and, in their closed and lovely faces, recognized the apparition of small household objects that had vanished in the wake of the twelve-day rain.

As things stood, though, husbands and girlfriends and elderly parents were excited beyond words to know that nights of uninterrupted sleep and considerably calmer days might await them, and months sooner than they'd been expecting, at that. And so, the women were welcomed into the homes of the expecting Foreston families with open arms and few, if any, questions asked.

XIV.

"You know, Sylvie, I never would've thought that adding another woman to this apartment would do any good," Amy remarked as she poured a cup of hot coffee, "but you have been absolutely amazing. How did you know we needed you so badly?"

The woman called Sylvie smiled as she took the cup Amy offered, never bringing the coffee to her lips. "I assumed that the local doctor could use some help, given how many women in town are due at the same time. Word gets around in our trade, and I thought to come by and see if my services would be beneficial."

"Well," Amy said, drinking her own mug of coffee and shaking her head, "I am so glad you did." She lowered her voice. "Honestly, I'd been hoping Miranda would have been set up in her own place by now. But since you've started staying with us, I feel like having her here with a baby wouldn't be the worst thing in the world, at least for a little while. It might be kind of nice to get to know this kid when it finally arrives."

"New lives are miraculous," Sylvie seemed to agree. "Some more than others, of course."

Amy shrugged. "I've never wanted to have a kid. I mean, labor just seems like too much to handle, and pregnancy, all those months...I don't want to feel like I'm renting out my body to a stranger, even if it's a baby. No offense or anything."

"None taken."

"Anyway..." Amy gestured to the cup in Sylvie's hands. "Did you need milk or sugar with that or something?"

Sylvie appeared to only remember the coffee after it had been pointed out. "Oh…I suppose I just don't drink things quite so hot as this."

Amy set her own empty mug in the sink. "I'm going to head to work. Do you think you can manage here by yourself for the day? I mean, like I said, you're a godsend, but it isn't so easy to handle some of Miranda's…feelings."

Sylvie laughed softly. "I promise you, that is very much my business. We'll be fine—you go ahead and go to work."

"Total godsend," Amy repeated, grabbing her purse and heading for the front door of the apartment. "Thanks again!"

"Of course."

After the door had closed, Sylvie walked over to the kitchen sink. She poured the coffee from her own cup down the drain, ran the tap to clean its remnants out, and then headed towards the second bedroom where Miranda was.

XV.

Max Orton was more than a little relieved when Simone first came to stay next door. Their neighbor's rages had terrified his children, and his wife found the sound of them disturbing. He'd even noticed that he felt frequently on edge, given the suddenness of the rants. It wasn't easy living close to such chaos, and having someone around to help calm things down was greatly appreciated.

Max couldn't understand why the woman was so inclined to her outbursts. Sure, Cecelia had had some rough moments with each of her three pregnancies, but nothing that involved throwing things and screaming into the night. He figured that every woman experienced things a little differently; he'd just had no idea how different it could get.

As the days passed, though, he found that he was starting to feel unsettled by Simone's presence. She was stunningly beautiful, and very strange—she didn't speak much, didn't seem interested in making friends around town, and she was always bringing bizarre new plants into their neighbor's place from who knew where.

But what was most uncomfortable for Max was the feeling that he knew the woman from somewhere, even though she was supposed to be from parts beyond Foreston. He couldn't put his finger on it, but everything about her, every minute detail—even the maroon dress she never seemed to take off, though she appeared impeccably tidy and the dress undoubtedly clean—all of it seemed etched somewhere deep in his memory.

"Simone," he called out one morning, noting that they were both leaving home at the same time, "you heading out for the day? Need a lift anywhere?"

"Thank you for the offer, but I'm fine, Mr. Orton," she replied, the placid smile on her face reaching nowhere near her dark, deep-set eyes. "I prefer to walk. I never know what I might encounter along my way."

He nodded as though this made perfect sense, though it didn't make any at all. "You can call me Max. Everything going all right over there with you folks?"

"We're doing just fine," she replied. "And how is your family? Your children are well?"

He nodded again, not knowing what to make of the woman. Beyond finding her unsettlingly familiar, he always experienced a nearly grotesque feeling when he spoke with her. She was attractive beyond any woman he'd ever encountered: gorgeous figure, stunning features, thick hair and a full mouth. But whenever he thought of bringing his lips to hers, the urge to retch rose up in his mouth so powerfully that one time, he almost did vomit on the spot. And he seemed to feel faint in her presence, as though something were being drained from him through the simple act of conversing with the woman.

"I'm glad to know they're all well, especially your wife." Simone punctuated this last remark with a dip in her tone that Max didn't understand.

"How's that?" he managed, wanting to get out of this little chat he'd initiated but, now that his head was spinning, not having any idea of how to do so.

"Mothers should be respected, always," she said, her dark gaze unwavering, and the light-headedness sang between Max's ears. "They are the bearers of so many things. Important things."

"Mmm." His tongue had grown fat in his mouth, and the world was swimming before his eyes.

"Well, I must get going, now," she told him, not waiting for him to say farewell in turn. "Do send my regards to your children's mother, Mr. Orton."

Max sat down heavily on his front porch and waited for the sickness that had overcome him to abate. What was it about Simone? Or could it be something else that was making him feel this way? He'd never wanted to cheat on Cecelia before. And, he realized, he didn't want to now—even the notion brought him back to that perfect, repulsive mouth. Perhaps thoughts of straying from his wife were what had set on his queasiness. Simone had mentioned respect, and though the conversation had been surreal, he knew on some level that she'd been right. Cecelia deserved his respect, at the very least, and much affection beyond that.

The impulse to kiss his wife became the most powerful thing he'd felt yet that morning, and it was the one emotion he decided ought to stay. He unlocked the front door of his home and went back inside, embracing a surprised Cecelia, who happily settled into her husband's arms.

"What's this about?" she murmured into his ear.

He only held her tighter, not knowing whether to say that he was grateful for her every day, or to tell her that he thought he might have almost died on the front porch just a moment ago, poisoned by thought and saved here and now by a simple act of love.

XVI.

Marie didn't miss Theo in the slightest. He'd moved in with his mother barely a week after Sirena had started taking care of her, and that was just fine with Marie—Sirena was a hell of a lot better at knowing what she needed than Theo had been.

"I just don't understand why he's been so useless lately," she complained to Sirena as the other woman rubbed warm oils into her swollen feet. "I mean, you're basically a complete stranger, and I know this is your job and everything, but you're taking care of me fine! Why couldn't he get it together?"

"Sometimes it's hard to know what a mother will need," Sirena told her soothingly, not looking up from the task at hand. "Some even say that only the being inside of her really knows what it is that she requires."

"Yeah, well," Marie gestured at her belly, "I don't even know how the kid got here in the first place. I was taking every precaution I could, and I damn well know that Theo wasn't trying to knock me up."

This seemed to give Sirena pause. "Are you not happy to be a mother?"

Marie sighed. "It's not that. I'm sure I'll be fine with everything once the baby's here. I don't know, I guess it all comes back to Theo. We've been together forever, you know, and I still have no clue if he ever plans on proposing. I mean, you saw how he is. Things get a little difficult, and where does he go? Straight to his mother's, like a kid himself. How is he going to be a father?"

"He might surprise you," Sirena offered. "Sometimes, when parenthood becomes a reality, it changes everything. He could come around."

"I guess."

"And you shouldn't get too upset," the other woman continued, taking a moment to pour a little more oil into her hand before returning to Marie's toes. "You need your spirits high so that you're healthy enough to bring someone into this world. It takes a lot of effort to create another being."

"You must know all about that, huh?" Marie shook her head, a wry smile on her face. "I never thought I'd buy into the whole midwife home-birth thing. It always seemed like a crock of weird tree-hugger shit to me, but you really do seem to know what you're doing."

"It's crucial that I do."

"Oh yeah? Why is that?"

Sirena's face tightened nearly imperceptibly. "I've seen lives forged in terrible ways," she replied quietly. "It's not enough to think you're going to bring someone into the world and expect things from her right away. That person needs a chance to form, to find herself."

Marie thought this over. "Yeah, even though I wasn't expecting to be a mom, I definitely don't want to be an asshole to my kid. Wait—you said 'she.' You think it's a girl?"

Sirena shrugged noncommittally, and Marie grinned. "I think she's a girl, too. I'd like a girl. That'll really drive Theo nuts, don't you think?"

Sirena smiled back. "I think any new life has the potential to wreak a bit of havoc, should she find herself so inclined."

XVII.

The last thing Mark Templeton had ever expected was to have a wife and a mistress both pregnant at the same time.

He knew for a fact that Adriana had been careful—they'd both taken precautions—and Miranda? He and Miranda had barely touched each other that year, had rarely been in the same room long enough to have a conversation, never mind make a baby. But somehow, he was about to be a father twice over.

Being sheriff had become much more exciting than he'd ever wanted it to be, too. He'd had wives and husbands nearly stabbed, run over, set on fire, attacked by guard dogs they didn't even know had been brought into the house—not to mention Miranda trying to blow his head off in bed that one night. He'd had to coordinate with fire and emergency services more often in the past weeks than he'd ever needed to do in his whole career. And at this point, he knew most of the hospital staff in Emergency by name. What the hell was happening to his sleepy little town?

Miranda had moved out, and Adriana had refused to move in. His home had become a sorry, unplanned bachelor pad, and it seemed like things between him and Adriana might be over for good. Some woman had moved into her place, probably a hippie or a psychic judging from the clothes she wore, and Adriana had refused him at the door the last time he'd gone to see her.

"I'm sorry, Mark, but I just don't know what to do with a man who got both me and his wife pregnant at the same time," she'd told him, shaking her head.

"You're acting like I did this on purpose!"

Adriana said nothing, just raised an eyebrow as she closed the door in his face.

"I'd have to be crazy!" he shouted through the door, but he could tell she'd already retreated into the apartment.

He had to figure out what was happening. It didn't seem like Foreston could keep blaming the twelve-day rain for all the strangeness—damn the weather, this was bigger than that! Women pregnant all over town, acting crazy and trying to kill everyone; other strange women moving in everywhere like a plague of New Age supermodels; and Mark, sitting here alone on a Friday, two babies on the way, with no woman to so much as share a meal with.

And after all, he was local law enforcement. It was his job to investigate when things were going wrong in his town, and things certainly weren't going right. If anyone was going to get to the bottom of this mess, it seemed like it would have to be him. And damnit, he wasn't about to run from the challenge.

"Jim," he said into his phone, calling one of his deputies. "You got some time to drop by tonight, man?...Yeah, work-related, but I'll pick up pizza and beer. Strange shit's been getting a little too strange, if you hear me...Yeah, that's right. All right then, see you in a couple hours."

XVIII.

If the Foreston sheriff intended to unravel the mystery that was working its way through his small town, he would have done well to set his sights on its outskirts. Of course, no one right away suspects that which is out of mind, and there wasn't much reason for the citizens of Foreston to think often of Artinand, if they thought of him at all. Beyond fixing watches and household items from times past, he had few dealings with the town and was mostly left to his solitude. And that, of course, was exactly the way he liked it.

But Artinand was now focused quite intently on what was happening in the heart of Foreston, and he'd finally come to a decision regarding his creations: he would seek them out and destroy them using the very kiln in which they'd been formed. If it had made them, it could end them, he reasoned. And besides, it seemed an appropriate end to such ill-made handiwork, wretches that had scorned him from the start and that were likely to draw unwanted attention from the town as a result of their recent antics.

Despite his somewhat extensive experience with crafting prophetic beings, it seemed that Artinand didn't understand their nature very well. And perhaps this was to be expected: one who does not think much of others will not necessarily think any differently towards his own progeny. In Artinand's mind, the sibyls were just as he'd last seen them. The idea that they might have transformed beyond his grasp and his workshop did not ever enter his thoughts.

So, as members of local law enforcement began to gather their resources in an effort to deduce what was the matter in Foreston, Artinand set out on a quest of his own. Both parties could have been said to be seeking a kind of retribution. They did not recognize that a web of vengeance had already been skillfully woven around them, and that they had been marked as prey by its shrewd and patient weavers.

XIX.

Jim Eaves looked skeptically at the evidence board in front of him at the sheriff's station. "I don't know, Mark. I mean, I get that stuff around town has been a little strange like we talked about, but do you really think all of this is…well, evidence? I mean, we can't exactly take any of it to court."

Mark had put together all of the information they'd discussed over beers at his place the week before, including the weird psychic incidents in Foreston that had come and gone almost overnight, the weirder pregnant ladies who seemed ready to kill anyone who crossed their paths, and even the weather that Mark was figuring might have somehow started things getting weird in the first place.

"I mean," Jim added, "we can't go after the weather."

"I'm not suggesting we do," Mark assured him. "But somebody's got to be behind all of this, Jimmy."

"You think? I mean, how do you get behind the rain?"

Mark sighed, and Jim wondered at his old friend's struggle to be patient with him when he was the one who had made the magical crime board they were looking at. Sheriff or not, a lot of these ideas were pretty out there.

"I'm talking about the fact that lives are being ruined," Mark went on. "Strange weather notwithstanding, you've got to admit that ruining lives is a pretty human thing to do."

"Well, I guess that's true," Jim allowed. He didn't want to argue with Mark too much. In addition to him being Jim's boss, Mark was a good buddy, and he was going through a rough patch, what with Miranda and the other woman both pregnant at the same time.

"So we've got the three major incidents that we talked about outlined across the board: the twelve-day rain, the psychic citizens, and the pregnancies."

Jim nodded in agreement. Doubtful though he was of some of the things that Mark was guessing at, he couldn't argue with what he'd witnessed with his own eyes. And having to pull a pregnant woman out of a tree from which she was throwing live firecrackers at her husband, well, that had done a bit to convince him. He also believed Mark's story about knowing that Miranda was going to shoot him that night—he'd gone over the scene at their house himself, and there was no way she could have missed if Mark hadn't known somehow that she was going to shoot where and when she did. Besides, Mark had never lied to Jim once in their long friendship.

"We've received several reports from around town," Mark continued, "and they vary a bit, but all of them point to one or more of these three incidents. But last night, I went through all our files, and I've come across one report and *only* one that stands out from all the others." Mark pointed to the right-hand side of the board where he'd pinned up a burglary report.

"What is it?" Jim asked, his curiosity now piqued.

"Erica Pierre called in what she described as a robbery/home invasion, though I didn't give it much thought as such at the time."

"Well, why not?" Jim prodded him. "Erica's not one to make a crank call."

"Because of what was missing. It was a single object that she'd kept on her mantelpiece, of little to no value beyond the sentimental."

Jim waited a beat, then rolled his eyes. "Man, cut the suspense and just tell me."

"Remember those little doll things that Artinand was selling for a while? He made a bunch of them and then sold them all around town?"

"Artinand, out on the edge of town? Fixes-watches Artinand? You really think he could be involved in this?"

Abandoning his lively presentation at the board, Mark sat in a chair across from Jim, his voice low and excited. "Think about it, Jimmy. The guy's a loner with little to no ties to the community. He barely lives in Foreston, out there in the middle of nowhere with no one else around."

"I'll remind you that *I* live alone in a quiet part of town."

Now Mark rolled his eyes. "Jim, come on—you know what I mean. You've got friends all over the place, never mind that you work here, serving your community. But Artinand's all by himself, he's unpleasant, and there's nobody he can claim even as an acquaintance. I mean, half the time you walk in that shop, he's shouting to himself about who knows what. Work with me here, buddy—he's a strange one and you know it."

Jim mulled this over for a bit. Mark wasn't wrong—Artinand was kind of a strange guy. He never showed at community functions, and if he did come into town, it was to run errands. He never hung around or talked to anybody, and it seemed pretty clear that he didn't want to be spoken to.

"Okay, I'll bite," he told Mark. "But what do you think he's done?"

"That, I don't know," Mark admitted. "I don't really have any ideas, either, except for that missing doll. Do you remember what he called them?"

Jim shook his head. "I can't say I do, but I'm pretty sure that Barbara Stillman had one."

"Stillman, Stillman…" Mark furrowed his brow, then shook his head. "Do I know her, Jimmy?"

"Probably by sight. She moved in next to the Argos sisters not all that long ago. She and her husband, John, had left Foreston when their son had gone off and had his family. They wanted to help him with the kids, so they moved—this was years ago. I think she got homesick when John died last year, and she was back in town shortly after."

"How the hell do you know all that?"

"I was seeing someone in the building for a bit," Jim said cryptically, and Mark grinned.

"Still don't kiss and tell, huh, Jimmy?"

"Never mind that." Jim cleared his throat. "Why don't I call Barbara and ask her about the doll?"

"Let's both ask her," Mark suggested, standing and grabbing the keys to his truck. "Come on—as long as no one else in town tries to shoot her husband or set her house on fire today, I'm sure we've got plenty of time to pay a visit."

XX.

Ivra Orton was coloring with sidewalk chalk in front of her home with her older brother, Thomas, when she noticed the two women approaching their neighbor's house.

"Who are they?" she asked Thomas in a low voice.

The boy glanced over his shoulder and shrugged. "I don't know." He quickly lost interest and returned to his drawing, the chalk mashing strangely into the rough concrete, as though someone had dampened it before giving it to the children to use.

But Ivra sat transfixed, the piece of blue chalk in her palm momentarily forgotten. As the two women walked gracefully up the path to the neighbor's house, she took in the sight of them: long, fluid clothing gracefully trailing behind them as they stepped along in unison. Some part of her registered, even at her young age, that she herself would never grow to be so beautiful, nor was she likely to encounter other women so striking in both appearance and manner.

"Why are they going next-door?" she pressed the issue, and her brother offered an exasperated sigh.

"Maybe they lost something." Thomas looked over at the house once again as Simone emerged through the front door. "Oh, they're Miss Simone's friends, see? They're probably just visiting her." He waved an arm, and called loudly, "Hi, Miss Simone!"

The three women seemed surprised to have been noticed, but as their eyes settled on the two children playing outside, they offered identical guarded smiles.

"Hello, Thomas," Simone called out, her voice bell-like as it moved across the properties on a cool breeze. "How are you today?"

"I'm fine," he answered with a grin. His sister remained silent, continuing to stare at the women.

"And you, Ivra? How are you?" This time, it was one of the other women who spoke. Her voice was as smooth as Simone's, almost enchanting in its gentle tone.

"How do you know my name?" Ivra asked when she finally felt brave enough to respond.

The women seemed to find this funny, and their smiles grew a little less cautious. "How could I not?" the one who'd spoken to her answered. "We know everyone's names. That's what good neighbors do, isn't it?"

"Well, what are your names?" Thomas asked a little coyly, apparently wanting to please these neighbors that, until a moment ago, he hadn't even known were his.

The two women introduced themselves as Sylvie, the one who had asked after Ivra, and Sabine. All three remained in front of the house next door as they spoke to the children; none made a move towards them.

"Do you want to come over and color with us?" Thomas offered, and out of habit, Ivra withdrew. She was shy, and she didn't like new adults. And besides, there was clearly something different about these women, and she didn't know what it was or what it meant.

"Thomas," she said to her brother in a half-whisper, "Mommy says we aren't supposed to talk to strangers."

"They're not strangers, they're neighbors," her brother retorted, rolling his eyes at her.

"It seems you both make good points," Sabine observed. "On the one hand, we are neighbors, as Thomas has articulated, and you should be polite to your neighbors."

"Indeed," Simone remarked, "though some people are less inclined towards good manners than others."

"On the other hand," Sabine continued, "your mother is wise to warn you to take caution around people you haven't met before. New people can be dangerous."

"As can people one knows intimately," Simone chimed in again.

"Yes," Sylvie spoke up, turning her attention away from the children and looking pointedly at her companions. "And to that end, shall we make our way inside?"

Simone nodded, and Ivra just barely heard her say in her silken voice, "There is much to be discussed."

"Goodbye, children," Sabine said, lifting a hand in parting as she made her way into the house.

"Bye!" Thomas called back, not looking up from the artwork to which he'd returned, having once again lost interest in the three women next-door.

Ivra sat with her thoughts for some time before eventually resuming her drawings. And though they were made with elementary skill and the few pieces of chalk she could weasel away from her brother, if a passerby were to look carefully, they would find where Ivra had been working a rendering of three women with strangely flowing garments scrawled across the damp pavement in front of the Orton home.

XXI.

By the end of that week, Mark Templeton had knocked on the doors of twelve Foreston residents who at one point in time had owned what he learned was called a sibyl. And in each case, the sibyl in question had mysteriously vanished from its owner's possession without leaving a clue as to where it had gone.

The difficult thing was pinning down exactly when the sibyls had disappeared. Apparently, no one had really noticed when they'd lost theirs, and some of the people Mark and Jim spoke with didn't even know they had misplaced one until they were asked if it was missing. And when Mark asked how you could lose something so unusual without realizing it, most people shrugged and blamed "all the craziness with the rain."

"It's got something to do with the weather, Jim, I'm telling you," he'd said as they had left yet another house empty-handed.

Jim had tried not to look as doubtful as he clearly felt, and Mark was having a hard time keeping his patience with his good friend and colleague. He knew what he was doing— he'd been the town sheriff long enough to have earned his stripes, and the sum of his experience said to always look to the evidence, and that was exactly what he was doing. And all the evidence pointed in three clear directions: the sibyls, Artinand, and the twelve-day rain.

But, he told himself as he drove home that evening, Jim was right about one thing: he couldn't approach a suspect with evidence based on strange weather. He might be able to go after Artinand in a small capacity, given that all of his creations had gone missing from their owners' homes: robbery charges, maybe, or even something along the lines of a conspiracy to dupe folks out of their money. But there was no guarantee charges like that would stick long enough to keep Artinand in custody while Mark and Jim figured out what was really happening. There wasn't much else to go on, and nobody they'd spoken to really seemed to miss the sibyls. And that was making things more difficult.

Mark was about to turn down his street when he decided, on a whim, to drive over to Amy's and see how Miranda was doing. The behavior of the pregnant women around town seemed to have quieted in recent weeks, which, it now occurred to him, might be another lead to look into. He hadn't yet done much investigation there—his gut still liked Artinand for this, and he didn't want to upset anyone with a pregnant wife at home. People got protective of pregnant women, and rightly so; he guiltily told himself that he was already a shit father, and neither of his kids had even been born yet.

But Mark figured if things really had gotten a little calmer as they seemed to have done, maybe he would have the chance to try and change that. He pulled up in front of Amy's apartment building and put the truck in park. It took him two deep, slow breaths before he was able to get himself out of the car.

When he knocked on the apartment door, neither Amy nor Miranda answered. "Can I help you, sheriff?"

The woman was a stunner: one of those supermodel hippies that had started showing up around town. She was a bit taller than Mark, something he wasn't sure any woman he'd ever met had been, and above her knockout figure was the sweetest, most striking face he had seen in his life.

He felt his cheeks redden, but the blood swiftly left them as he reminded himself of his current situation: two babies on the way with two different women. You might not be able to teach an old dog new tricks, but Mark wasn't all that old, and he certainly wasn't gunning for kid number three.

He cleared his throat. "Hello, ma'am. Is Miranda at home?"

"She is," the woman said, not moving to let him inside.

"Can I…may I come in and see her?" For some reason, he felt he needed to be particularly polite with this woman, though why that was he couldn't have explained.

"You might," she went on, still standing in the doorway. "But do you think that Miranda wants to see you?"

He was annoyed by his own flustered response to this Amazonian stranger. Who was she to keep him from the mother of his child, his own wife? But even knowing that he was law enforcement and this was a random hippie from who knew where, and that all aspects of the situation said he had the upper hand, it still took him several moments to reply to her. "Uh…ma'am, I'm the father of Miranda's baby, and I…"

"I know who you are, of course, sheriff," came the cool response. "And I'm not here to get in the way of any investigation you might be conducting. But as Miranda's midwife, I do have to ensure the health and happiness of my client. Can you understand that?"

"Well, sure, but—"

"Now, I'm more than happy to continue speaking with you, but I'm afraid I can't let anyone inside while Miranda is resting, as she happens to be at the moment. It's crucial that

Melissa Bobe

she is not disrupted at this stage of the pregnancy. Shall I come outside and speak with you further?"

Her voice never grew louder, and the placid evenness of her expression never altered, but there was something in Mark that responded to her offer to come out of the apartment as if it were a very real threat of violence. In spite of himself, he absolutely recoiled at the thought of spending even another moment with this woman.

"You know what? I was just checking up on her and the baby," he backtracked, trying and failing to smile nonchalantly. "But if they're fine…?"

"I assure you, sheriff, I have not been negligent in my duties for a moment," she said, a small smile playing on her lips. "Miranda's pregnancy is progressing beautifully."

"Great, that's…that's perfect. Thank you."

"But are you sure I can't help you with anything else?" she pressed him. "No police matters that you're currently at work on?"

If he hadn't wanted to get away from the woman so badly, Mark might have challenged the tone with which she'd just spoken, which he swore was ever so slightly mocking. And to ask about active investigations, well, that was suspicious, to say the least.

But that discomfort he felt wasn't diminishing, and though he cursed himself in his mind, aloud he replied, "Not at all, ma'am. You have a good night."

"Goodnight, sheriff."

XXII.

When Artinand caught sight of the sheriff and deputy coming up the road to his shop, he was more annoyed than surprised. He had known there was a chance that the sibyls would somehow implicate him to the townspeople before he could get to them.

But he had been going through his library, all of the alchemical and mechanical and mystical texts that had informed his creations, and he still hadn't found what he wanted just yet. There was much more written in his books about animating curious objects than there was information on how to stop them, and that was presenting a real challenge. While he was nearly certain that the kiln would be sufficient, Artinand was meticulous, if nothing else. It was how he'd built his professional reputation, and he didn't typically settle for less than perfect confidence in all aspects of his work.

As for the immediate moment, he decided to go out the back entrance and avoid the law entirely. He didn't think much at all of the Foreston authorities, and the last thing he needed to do was make small talk while they looked around his shop and got whatever ideas about him their feeble intellects might be capable of. And besides, while he wasn't finished with his research, he'd decided that it was time to start locating the sibyls. He had a vague sense of a handful of townsfolk he might have sold some to, and he would eventually find the rest. He set out through the back door towards the park that separated his home from the central part of the town.

Artinand wasn't interested in making eye contact or saying hello as he made his way through Foreston; he had mostly disregard and in some cases outright disdain for all who lived there, given their apparent contentment with their small lives. He tended to walk at a brisk pace, hands in his pockets and gaze on the ground before him, avoiding niceties at all costs.

He didn't notice right away, as he began navigating a street he believed one of his customers might live on, that his presence had drawn the attention of a figure seated in the second-floor window of a small red house. But even a focused man will eventually feel a gaze if it burns hot enough upon his back. Uneasily, Artinand glanced around at the homes on the quiet street until his eyes eventually landed on the window and figure in question.

It takes a lot to shake a bitter old soul who has written off most of daily living as banal and beneath him. The sight of one of his creations come to life, however, nearly bowled Artinand over. There was no doubt that it was her, the sibyl he'd shaped in the hopes of discerning how the world as all knew it would end. She wore the same midnight-colored robe and long tresses he'd adorned her with, and her face, though now flesh instead of ceramic, was exactly as he'd so carefully crafted it.

He stood, rooted to the spot, gawking at her in shock and, eventually, dismay: no kiln would destroy this aberration, this moving, breathing thing that had once been only too easy to grasp in his fist. He might have remained there, staring, had she not begun to smile wickedly at him, mocking his futility. The moment he caught the expression, Artinand spat violently on the ground, and she raised an eyebrow, still smiling, before closing the curtains and retreating into the house.

So they had changed, then. He stomped his way through Foreston, swearing under his breath and agitatedly pumping his fists in his pockets, not caring that he drew the attention of those he passed in his muttering, erratic rage. The clever bitches had taken human form, had they? Well, he told himself, then they could be reckoned with like humans.

When he returned home, he made sure that the sheriff's truck was gone before he walked over to a shed on his property that was shut with a rusted lock. It took a bit of tugging to pry open, given how rare it was that Artinand unlocked it, but it eventually gave way with a muted click. He stepped inside the shed and rustled around for several minutes until he found what he was looking for.

As evening fell on Foreston and Artinand made his way back inside his home and workshop, the clouds in the sky parted, revealing a bone-white half-moon shining above the cold, damp town. Its silver light reflected off the edge of a polished blade, the hilt of which Artinand had gripped firmly in one of his angry fists.

XXIII.

Having slowly made her way to answer the door, her feet swollen and tender as she neared the end of her pregnancy, Brenna Keith was surprised to find Mark Templeton standing on her front porch.

"Well, you're a sight for sore eyes!" She hugged him warmly. Mark and Brenna had been great friends back in high school, and though their busy lives ensured they hadn't seen each other nearly so often as she would have liked over the years, their reunions were always happy.

"You look beautiful," he told her, shaking his head as he regarded her. "I didn't realize you were also expecting."

"That's right," she suddenly remembered aloud. "I heard...don't you have two on the way?" He shrugged sheepishly, and Brenna laughed. "Come on in. I was just about to microwave some popcorn and dump M&Ms all over it—the kids are at a friend's place for a sleepover, and I don't feel nearly as guilty eating crap if they're not around to see it. Care to join me?"

"Sounds heavenly." Mark stepped inside the house and offered his arm for Brenna to lean on as they made their way into the kitchen. "Where's Xiomara?"

"Oh, she and Selene ran out to get more snacks and some bath salts for me to soak my feet in. The further along I get, the hungrier I am, but I guess a body can only bloat up so much without giving its owner a little hell."

Mark paused, seeming to choose his words carefully as he sat down at the kitchen table. "Is Selene a friend of yours?"

"She's a saint," Brenna replied, putting the popcorn in the microwave and joining him at the table. "She's been helping us get ready for the baby, and when I go into labor, she's going to deliver it."

"Really," Mark said flatly. "Let me guess—she's tall, beautiful, and has absolutely no sense of humor."

Brenna burst out laughing again. "Impending fatherhood has certainly made you a grim one! But I guess that's a fair description of Selene. Why, have you bumped into her in town or something?"

Mark shook his head, then gazed at Brenna seriously. "Are you sure she's who she says she is?"

She sighed. "Mark, it's not that I don't appreciate the visit, but what is this about? Is it because of things with you and Miranda? Because I know it must be a really hard time, and—"

"No, no, this isn't about Miranda. Brenna, what do you actually know about this woman?"

"I know all our problems just about vanished from the moment she came to stay with us," Brenna said. She put a hand on her stomach and gave a little smile. "I know that I was terrified to have this baby until she showed up."

"You? Terrified?" He made a face of mock disbelief. "This from the girl who kicked my ass at homecoming just to prove she could?"

"I wish I were still like that." Her voice turned sad. "Truth is, I wasn't even sure I wanted to try for a third baby. Xiomara and the kids were all excited, but I didn't know if I could do it again. And the doctor wasn't all that optimistic that it would even take."

Mark nodded. "What changed?"

"I don't know." Brenna's gaze drifted off into the distance. "I just wasn't sure I could start over with another baby—the late nights, the teething, my body being beat to shit all over again. It's not like I don't already have a family to take care of. And the first part of the pregnancy was just awful. I didn't have such a rough go of it with Nate or Angie, but this time I was completely miserable. I felt insane."

"You weren't one of the fire department calls, were you?"

She chuckled. "I heard about that. No, I think having the kids in the house kept me just this side of homicidal. But I can't say I wasn't thinking about hurting myself."

"Bren—"

She shook her head, waving the thought away. "I got over it."

"You're strong, Brenna. Of course you pulled through."

Her whole face brightened. "Well, Selene came to stay with us, and she just took care of everything. I mean, she was amazing—from the moment she arrived, it was like she knew what I needed before even I did. And it wasn't just me, either—the kids love her, and I know Xiomara is so grateful for the help. She was exactly what the whole house needed."

"That does sound pretty incredible," he remarked, but his face remained serious.

Brenna continued, "And now, I just feel so at peace getting ready for the baby. Xiomara and the kids are happy again, and I'm totally relaxed. The nerves are gone, and I'm just excited that we're about to have another awesome kid to raise."

The microwave beeped loudly, alerting them that the popcorn was done. Mark helped Brenna to her feet, and she took out a large red bowl and started pouring popcorn in before reaching for a bag of chocolate candy.

"So then, this woman Selene," Mark said, leaning against the kitchen counter and stealing a kernel of popcorn from the bowl, "she's legit? You've seen her midwife papers, or whatever?"

Brenna snorted. "Ever the skeptic. Listen, if you're so suspicious, stay another fifteen or twenty minutes. They'll be back by then, and you can interrogate her yourself, *sheriff.*" She punched him teasingly in the arm.

He grinned and rubbed the place she'd hit as though he were wounded, but then his smile faded. "I can't stay, Bren. I just wanted to know that you're all right."

"More than all right, Mark." She squeezed his shoulder affectionately, as if to apologize for the punch. "I'm fantastic."

"Well, good." He straightened up. "You sit back down and relax some more. I can see myself out."

"What about you?"

"What about me?" he returned.

Brenna gave him a knowing look. "Are *you* all right, Mark?"

He kissed her on the cheek. "I'll see you soon. Can't wait to meet the new kid."

"Hey!" she called as he started to leave the kitchen. "Why'd you stop by? I mean, if you didn't know I was pregnant…?"

"Oh." He turned around to face her again. "I wanted to ask: didn't your mom have one of those little ceramic sibyls that Artinand made?"

She thought for a minute, then nodded. "Yeah, the little weird doll? I'm pretty sure she bought one off him when she went to have my grandfather's watch fixed. That was a while ago."

"Does she still have it?"

Brenna thought for another moment. "Honestly? I don't know. In addition to having a bad case of baby brain, it's not really something that I would notice with all the stuff she has lying around. I could call and ask her when she gets back next week—she and Dad went for a vacation to prepare for the baby."

"How's that?"

"They figure that if baby sitting's anything like it was with the first two, they'd like to get some fun in before all that starts."

Mark left laughing, and Brenna sat to enjoy her popcorn. It was strange seeing her old friend again so suddenly, but the visit had been nice, even if hadn't lasted very long. She looked forward to telling Xiomara and Selene about it when they got back home.

XXIV.

Ruth Clancy couldn't quite explain what was wrong with the ultrasound machine to the company representative on the other end of the line.

"Like I said, we were doing just fine with it," she told the man, who had been confused by what she'd described the first time. "Dr. Bronston had a patient with mobile gallstones just a couple of weeks ago, and we could see those perfectly. The imaging was just as it should have been. But when we took a look at the pregnancy this week, well, it's like I told you— there was nothing but a strange, bright, glowing light on the screen where the baby should have been."

The representative from the medical equipment company assured her that it didn't sound like any malfunction he'd ever heard of, and he asked once again if the doctor knew how to properly use the machine.

Frustrated with repeating herself and having to defend her employer, Ruth quickly said, "You know what, we'll just have to try again. Thanks for your time." And she hung up with a small, exasperated sigh.

Ruth was a dedicated employee, and most of the time, she truly loved her job. She liked being the kind face that greeted people when they weren't feeling their best. She enjoyed bumping into patients around town and having a pleasant conversation about what was going on in their lives. She loved seeing the children Dr. Bronston brought into the world grow into young adults who were still glad for the lollipop she offered on their way out of the office. And she was happy in the knowledge that she worked for a good, upstanding man who respected her and was grateful for her service, just as the town was grateful for his.

But the past few months had been more than a little trying, even for a devoted worker like Ruth. Dr. Bronston had been feeling slighted by several of the women in Foreston—specifically, by the twenty women who were due to have their babies very soon. They had all hired midwives, it seemed. And while at first Dr. Bronston had been relieved to know that the spike in pregnancies came with a commensurate surge in local prenatal caregivers, he quickly began to feel that, rather than being helped, he was being replaced.

The worst development yet had occurred just the other day. Dr. Bronston had managed to talk one patient into coming in for an ultrasound, just as a precaution. It had taken no small amount of coaxing, too—the doctor had had to make the phone call to secure the appointment himself. "Marie, please—I've known you since *you* came into this world, when I delivered you as a healthy baby girl. Please just come in so we can have a look and double-check that everything is fine. Let your old doctor have some peace of mind."

And then, of course, when the girl finally did come in to see the doctor, the ultrasound machine had gone and malfunctioned. No matter what Dr. Bronston had done, the stupid thing wouldn't work. Ruth tried to get the girl to reschedule on her way out, but it was no use—the damage had been done, and Marie didn't even wait around to pick out a lollipop. She just handed over her copay and left without another word.

Dr. Bronston was usually an even-tempered man, but he'd been in a foul mood ever since, and Ruth didn't know what she was going to tell him now that she'd struck out with the manufacturer. She wasn't used to the disharmony that had filled the office lately, and she didn't like it one bit.

She sighed again and dug into her stash of lollipops for a lime-flavored one. Today, she needed candy more than the patients did.

XXV.

It didn't take much snooping around for Artinand to figure out that there were twenty newcomers to Foreston in all, and that those twenty newcomers were residing in the homes of the pregnant women who months ago had been causing chaos around town. Learning the identities of the expectant mothers was a little more difficult; small talk wasn't his strong suit, and it wasn't something his customers anticipated when they entered his shop with whatever broken gadgets they needed fixed.

But despite the soggy nature of their perpetually damp town, the residents of Foreston were inclined to be friendly enough with one another. And so while Artinand's sudden interest in pleasant conversation was certainly unexpected, it would not have occurred to most people to regard it with concern or suspicion. Out of habit, they responded in kind, and Artinand found himself with heaps of exactly the kind of tedium he'd spent his entire life avoiding.

From these encounters, he had been able to deduce where at least ten of the sibyls were hiding, and he felt that was more than enough information for him to begin his mission to bring his creations to ruin. He was sure that he would be able to extract the location of the others from those he already knew how to find, and any plan had to be better than chatting with the dolts of Foreston for yet another day. He set out, dagger tucked into his belt and hidden beneath a light jacket, and began knocking on doors.

For whatever reason, though, he kept finding that the midwives of these households were not at home when he asked for them. Some had gone out to run errands, according to their clients; others had taken their daily walk and weren't expected home anytime soon. One had even gone to pick up the family's other children at school.

With each door that closed, Artinand's agitation grew. They were so clever, weren't they, his precognitive poppets, the fruits of his bitter labor. They could see him coming a mile away.

He was so frustrated by the time he visited the last household on his list that he didn't even bother with a pretense of neighborly interest, and sarcastic condescension dripped from his voice as he spoke to one Brenna Keith. Familiar enough with Artinand's reputation for odd behavior, Brenna wouldn't have thought much of the encounter had she not glimpsed the blade of a knife under his coat as he whirled off her doorstep and went on his way. That, combined with the fact that his name had come up in her surprise visit from the sheriff the week before, was enough for her to tell her wife about the incident. And Xiomara didn't waste a moment calling Mark Templeton and reporting what had happened.

As for Artinand, he once again stormed bitterly from the center of Foreston to its outskirts. He was too enraged to keep from cursing openly to himself about his creations, and damned anyone who would cross his path as he made his way home. No one did interfere with him directly, but the sheriff's office received three phone calls about behavior that was unusually agitated, even for Artinand.

And, unbeknownst to Artinand and those people who had observed him yelling on the street, his antics had garnered the attention of some other significant bodies. Twenty figures shadowed his path at a distance of several hundred feet, unnoticeable but quietly determined as they steadily followed him back to his house.

Once inside his workshop, Artinand did the unusual and broke out a bottle of whiskey. He preferred to keep his head clear most of the time, but he also wasn't used to coming up against such blatant failure, particularly in what he viewed as a battle of metaphysical wits. The sibyls were *his*, and how dare they evade him and mock his efforts at every turn! They were his to destroy just as they had been his to make, and he vowed that when morning came, he would figure out a way to find them and make them pay for his misery.

"Spiteful shrews," he snarled viciously, flecks of spit and whiskey flying from his lips. "Useless, selfish whores."

He eventually slid from his seat to the floor and there began dozing, his head lolling forward on his chest as he snored. In his drunken slumber, he didn't feel the ground beneath him, which like most of the floors in Foreston had lost the original strength of its foundations, begin to shift. He didn't notice as the tiles began to crumble and the floor slowly but surely started to sink, with him at its center. When his body had been trapped in wet concrete and broken ceramic up to his chest, he snorted wetly, but still didn't wake.

What finally did get Artinand's attention was a soft female voice that rang like a bell in the dead, dank air of his workshop. "Hello, Father."

His eyes opened with a start, and he sneered at the statuesque figure towering over him. "You've come to get me first, is that it? You ungrateful bitch."

She seemed to consider him for a long, quiet moment. "That's a strange thing to say, isn't it, Father? For what should we feel gratitude? For the curses and hatred and threats you've volleyed at us since we were conceived? Or for your new intentions to bring us to ruin?"

"You were made for *me*! To serve *me*!" His voice ripped from his throat in his rage, almost beastlike in its growling timbre. "And what do you do? Grant the gift of futuresight to every half-wit and inbred moron in this town of simple pissants!"

"Oh, we'll have to disagree on that, Father," the sibyl replied as she gracefully seated herself on a nearby stool, crossing her long legs at the ankles and folding her hands in her lap. "My sisters and I have found Foreston to be a special place, full of some very special people. It is our home, after all."

"You have no home!" he spat. "You're abominations. Do you think this town will make you any more welcome than it did me?"

"It already has," she said, smiling fondly as she looked out the workshop window that faced towards the center of Foreston. "We were taken out of this hellish place and into its citizens' homes, and when we returned in our new forms, we again were invited with open arms. And we're about to become much more permanent residents."

"What's that supposed to mean?" he snarled.

"It means," she replied, turning her gaze back to Artinand, the smile she had worn when speaking of the people of Foreston now completely gone, "that we will no longer have need to call you our father. And you will reap your just rewards, the gifts of fate that you've always felt so entitled to."

"Cryptic monster, say what you mean!"

"I mean what I say, Father." She stood again, casting her eyes down at him. "Don't you remember what future you intended me to reveal?"

He studied her for a moment, trying to imagine her as she had been when she was ceramic and grasped in his sweating hand. "You were to let me glimpse my own future," he finally replied. "My fate."

She smiled again, though with none of the warmth she had before. "That's right, Father. And that's exactly what I've come to do." She walked to the door.

"Where are you going?" he roared at her retreating form. "You can't leave me here!"

"But I must," she said as she opened the door. "Can't you see it, Father? I'm to leave you to your fate." And without another word, she was gone.

Artinand began screaming, and even on the outskirts of Foreston, it was likely that a passerby might have eventually heard him, had not the circle of twenty women around his home raised their hands all at once. As they lifted their arms and eyes to the evening sky, so the heat in the kiln that had made them began to rise.

Smoke and fumes began to pour out of the kiln, filling Artinand's workshop. The sheriff would have probably seen it trailing from the one open window—he was en route to Artinand's at that very moment—but he received a call that made him swerve into a U-turn and race in the other direction, towards a particular apartment in the town.

As the twenty figures who had gathered around the tinker's workshop quickly made their way back into Foreston, where twenty expectant mothers had started to call out for them, Artinand's terrified eyes reflected the fate that had finally revealed itself to him, a man who had wanted nothing more than to know what was to come.

XXVI.

"What do you mean, *they're all in labor?*"

Ruth had to hold the phone a few inches away from her ear as Dr. Bronston began shouting in incredulity. She'd gone back to the office late that evening when she realized that her wallet had slipped out of her purse inside of the desk drawer she kept it in. When she arrived, she saw the message light on the desk phone blinking, and was halfway through listening to the several reports of the onset of labor when the phone began to ring again.

"The midwives are all on duty, and from what the families are telling me, everyone's doing rather well," Ruth explained between exclamations on the other end of the line. "Really, Dr. Bronston, most of them called as a courtesy, but everyone seems to be fine." This resulted in further unintelligible exclamations, and Ruth, who in her many years of service had never found reason to lose patience with her employer, decided that it would be best for their working relationship if she just went ahead and hung up on him.

And fine the residents of Foreston were indeed. While the confused doctor paced his living room, trying to figure out which home to rush to first and where he was least likely to be turned away at the door, twenty families around town were preparing to grow larger by a soul. The sibyls had made their way back to their respective clients in plenty of time, and the labors were progressing along smoothly.

Each midwife performed her duties diligently, with family and friends standing by to support the mothers-to-be. Aside from the excited shouts at his secretary from Dr. Bronston, there was relatively little concern raised among those who knew that all of the infants would be arriving on the same night.

Only Mark Templeton found himself with a real problem, but he promised both expectant mothers that he would drive back and forth between them all night if he had to. Miranda and Adriana were considerably preoccupied and didn't care all that much what Mark was doing, given the pain they were both in, but Miranda's friend Amy managed to remind him that he was a fucking idiot as he passed her in the kitchen on one such trip between the mothers of his coming children.

For his part, Mark felt like he absolutely was the biggest idiot on the planet, but a happy and excited idiot at that. And as he drove with lights flashing and sirens blaring between the two homes, he decided that perhaps he could be a better father than he was a romantic partner, after all.

The labors ended at midnight. It was with great joy that twenty new babies were received into the arms of those loved ones standing by, their small cries ringing out in the perpetually damp night air of Foreston with no stars visible in the haze above to greet them.

As soon as mother and baby were settled and onlookers sighing their joy at the sight, the sudden absence of each midwife who had otherwise been so present and helpful became apparent. No matter how the families called out and searched for those strangers who had lived with them and kept their homes calm and happy in the previous months, the twenty women who had come to Foreston were now nowhere to be found.

Each of the mothers, however startled she might be by this disappearance, was not without gratitude for the midwife who had tended to her when she had needed it the most. And so it was that every one of the twenty new daughters of Foreston was named for the beautiful lady who had lived in her home until her arrival. And though the town never guessed where those mysterious visitors might have disappeared to, many close to the families of the infants saw a curious resemblance reflected in the lovely faces of the babies that the midwives had delivered.

XXVII.

Mark Templeton was so caught up in fatherhood that he'd forgotten for almost an entire day that he was also the town sheriff. He'd visited both of his daughters, Sylvie and Septima, throughout the night they were born and into the next, and he was deliriously exhausted and thrilled, all at the same time.

He received a call from Xiomara telling him that Brenna had also delivered their daughter, and that was when Mark remembered that Artinand had been spotted not long ago, shouting at no one and roaming around town with a knife.

His protective instinct stronger than it had ever been previously, Mark decided right away that this was a matter of great urgency. He called Jim, knowing it would be safer if he wasn't alone, given that he hadn't slept at all since becoming a father.

Jim embraced him heartily when he arrived outside of Amy's apartment, where Mark stood by his truck, looking fatigued but proud. "Well, I'll be goddamned—a father twice over, both girls, and in the same night! I don't know whether to congratulate you or to help you get started on your last will and testament."

Mark lifted his keys. "Do us one better and drive the truck for me. I don't know how well I'll handle behind the wheel, given the night I had."

"No kidding," Jim chuckled as he took the key ring from Mark's hand and they both got into the truck. "Now, are you sure that Artinand really had a knife on him?"

"Well, Brenna was sure, and plenty of people reported seeing him running around town, much more agitated than usual."

Jim shook his head. "I guess you were right to suspect him. Still, it seems strange that he'd snap all of a sudden when he's lived in town quietly for so long. You're sure that the pregnancy wasn't messing with Brenna's head at all?"

"I think she was as bad as the others, at first," Mark mused, his tired eyes closed as Jim drove them along to the edge of town. "But I saw her not all that long ago, and she was lucid as could be—completely normal, from what I could tell."

"Brenna Keith's always been sharp," Jim relented. "If she says she saw it, I'm inclined to believe it."

They pulled into the driveway of Artinand's home and saw that the lights in his workshop were out.

"That's strange," Jim remarked as they got out of the truck. "It's not that late, and he's always working on something in there."

They approached cautiously, and Mark peeked in a window. "Jim!" he cried suddenly. "Kick it down!"

Without hesitation, the deputy kicked in the front door of the workshop, and both men ran in. It wasn't until they got close to the body that they realized it was too late.

"How in the hell did he fall through the floor?" Jim wanted to know, letting out a low whistle as he crouched down to examine the scene.

Mark considered the body for a long moment, walking carefully around his deputy on the uneven, broken floor. "It's almost like the earth opened and swallowed him up."

"Well, he wasn't the nicest guy around, but I wouldn't wish this on anyone," Jim said. "You want me to go ahead and call the coroner to come get him, or do you think we need to run some more forensics in here first?"

Mark looked around the workshop, at the tools and the half-finished projects on the tables, the many strange books on the shelves, and the dust that had settled over everything in sight. "No ties to anyone means no grudges, either," he finally decided. "I don't think this is foul play so much as an act of nature. It's sad, but at least we don't have to break the news to anyone—Artinand never married, and he didn't leave any children behind."

"All right, then. I'll get Brian down here." Jim dialed the coroner and walked out onto the front steps to make the call.

Giving Artinand's corpse a final glance, Mark followed Jim out, letting the screen door of the house slap loudly behind him, the sound echoing with strange finality in the damp Foreston air.

Acknowledgements

Many wonderful people have supported me as a writer and made endeavors like *Sibyls* possible. I am happy to express here just how much their encouragement has meant.

Thank you to my dear friends for always rooting for me and helping me realize dreams like this book. A special shout-out of gratitude to Rachel Altvater, Carmen Cabello, Amy Hayman, Kate Schnur, and Alene Scoblete for being so generous with your time by reading *Sibyls* before publication.

When I announced that *Sibyls* would be entering the world, I received incredible support from an especially bookish corner of my life. To my classmates in the Queens College Master's in Library Science program and my colleagues at the Seaford Public Library and the Rockville Centre Public Library: thank you so much for the love! I'm thrilled to be able to say that I work with the best of the book-obsessed world.

I dedicated this novella to the creative people I've met on my writing journey, and I'd like to thank some of them here. To the New York City chapter of National Novel Writing Month, and to our fearless leader Grant Faulkner, thank you for this beautiful and welcoming community of writers. Special thanks to Kris and Audri for the bear hugs on the day I brought home my galleys. So much gratitude to Alexis Daria for offering wisdom and kindness from the very first day we met, for teaching me how to contribute meaningfully to this community, and for saving my quote reveal. To Yin Chang's 88 Cups of Tea podcast and storyteller community: you are a vibrant and inspiring bunch, and I know this book would not have come into existence without the podcast. Yin, I always have gratitude in my heart for all that you do for writers. To Brian Mooney of Storymatic Studios, thank you for the generosity, warmth, and enthusiasm you put into all of the work you do for your fellow creatives.

To the ladies of the Writing Hive, thank you for sharing your creative journeys with me. It has been a gift to get to know each of you, and I appreciate you letting me spam your inboxes! Special thanks to Shifa Kapadwala for your guidance on the industry, your friendship, and being a shining light in this world. Gratitude to the Twitter writing community, especially those of you who join us each week for Word Magic Chat. Tuesday nights would be absolutely no fun without you!

Sara Carrero and Eva Papka are responsible for this novella. Like the rest of my writing, it could not have happened without their willingness to read drafts and revisions, their sage advice, their support, and their delightful company. I could not have asked for better partners in crime than the two of you: you're both pure magic, and I am humbled and honored that I get to say I am in a writing group with you. I look forward to every manuscript yet to come.

I am fortunate to have been raised by two people who encouraged my love of writing and who have seen me through good and difficult times. Mom and Dad, no matter how I grow as a creative individual, I won't have adequate words to express all you've done for me. Thank you for always offering love and faith in my ability as a writer, and for letting me read you drafts of *Sibyls* around many evening cups of coffee.

Danny, I never hoped that I'd find the person whose soul mine would recognize immediately as its mate, but here we are. To the best cat dad, cookie chef, manga critic, chess wiz, and partner in love and in life I'll ever know: thank you for always believing in me, especially when I'm struggling to believe in myself. I've dared to hope my writing will reach readers because of you.

About the Author

Melissa Bobe is a speculative fiction writer and a children's librarian. She taught college writing and literature for the better part of a decade while earning two Master's degrees and a PhD in English literature, as well as an MFA in creative writing. Currently, she is a New York City Municipal Liaison for National Novel Writing Month and the organizer of The Writing Hive, a networking project for women who write or advocate for writers. She also cohosts a weekly Twitter event with her critique partners called Word Magic Chat, which is dedicated to discussions of writing and fantasy. Melissa's obsessions beyond writing include ballet, beekeeping, cats, cooking, and coffee, not necessarily in that order. *Sibyls* is her first published book, but it won't be her last.

abookbumble.com